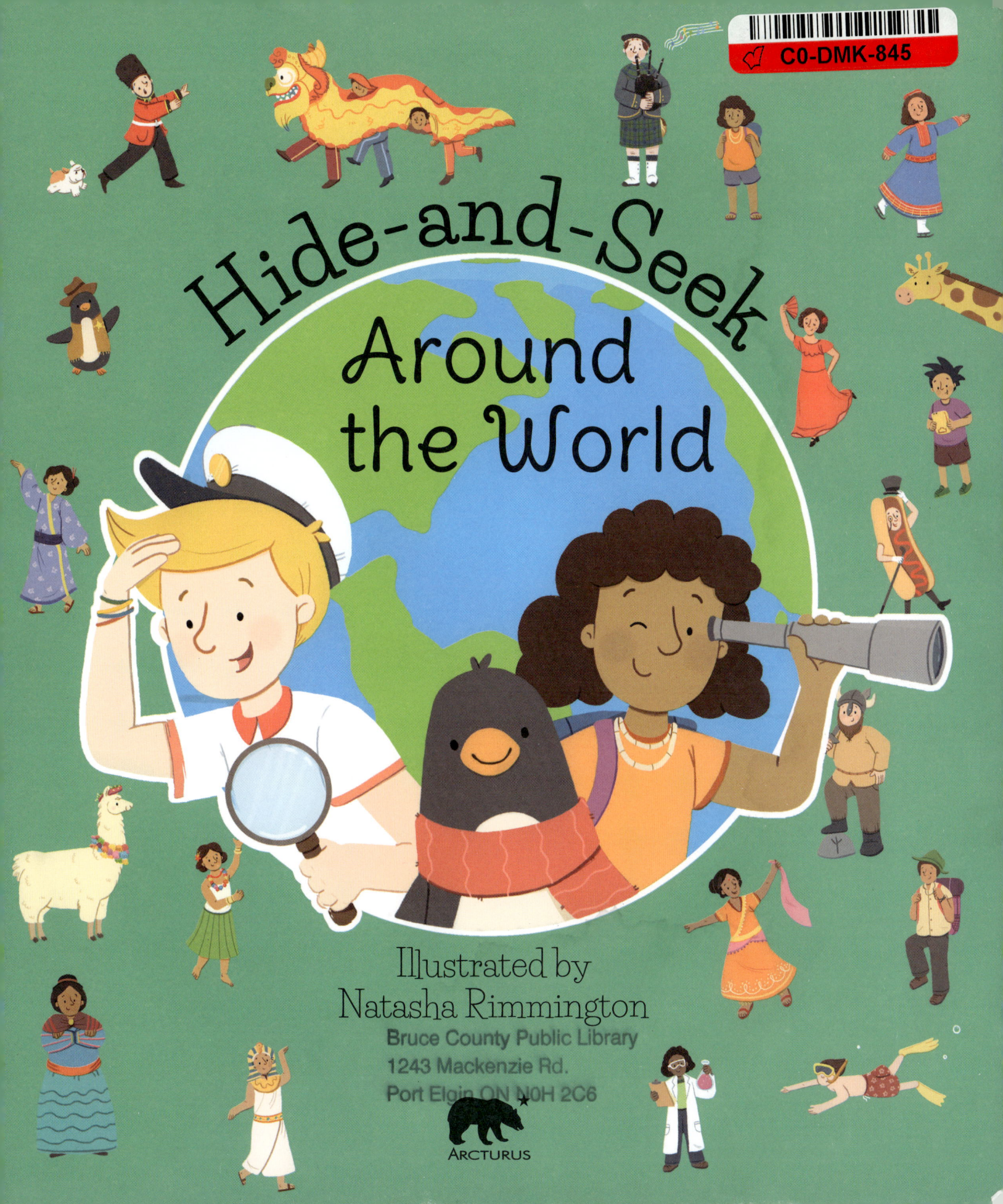

ARCTURUS

This edition published in 2021 by Arcturus Publishing Limited
26/27 Bickels Yard, 151–153 Bermondsey Street,
London SE1 3HA

Copyright © Arcturus Holdings Limited

All rights reserved. No part of this publication may be reproduced, stored in a retrieval system, or transmitted, in any form or by any means, electronic, mechanical, photocopying, recording, or otherwise, without prior written permission in accordance with the provisions of the Copyright Act 1956 (as amended). Any person or persons who do any unauthorized act in relation to this publication may be liable to criminal prosecution and civil claims for damages.

Author: Violet Peto
Illustrator: Natasha Rimmington
Designer: Rosie Bellwood
Design Manager: Jessica Holliland
Editorial Manager: Joe Harris

ISBN: 978-1-83940-625-6
CH008254NT
Supplier 29, Date 0221, Print run 10189

Printed in China

Let the Games Begin!

"Hi, I'm Sasha!"

"I'm Olly. And this is our penguin pal, Pertwee."

These three friends are hide-and-seek champions! Now they face the ultimate challenge in a global game of hide-and-seek, competing against masters of concealment from around the world. They have invited YOU to join their team and help them on their amazing adventure!

_____ is cordially invited

to join

Sasha, Pertwee, and Olly

in an international game of hide-and-seek.

So come and navigate the canals of Amsterdam as you search for Vincenza Van Gotcha, explore the ancient pyramids of Egypt while you hunt for Clever Cleo, and celebrate Chinese New Year in Shanghai on the lookout for Secretive Shuchun.

Do you have the observation skills to spot the world's greatest hide-and-seekers? Turn the pages to find out!

Fashionistas in France

Bonjour! Welcome to Paris, the city of love, fashion, and art. Can you find Claudette LaCacheuse hiding near the Eiffel Tower?

Claudette

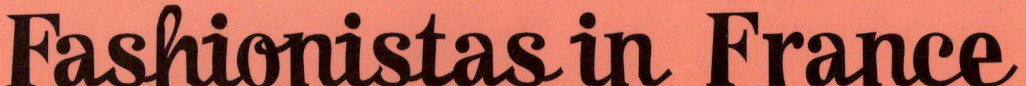

Party in Portugal

This happy couple have tied the knot at the beautiful Pena Palace. Look out for Cunning Carlos among the wedding guests.

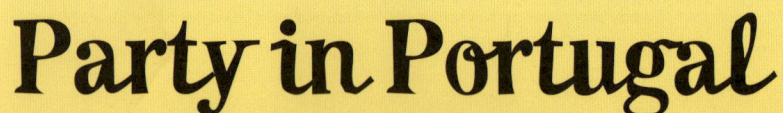
Carlos

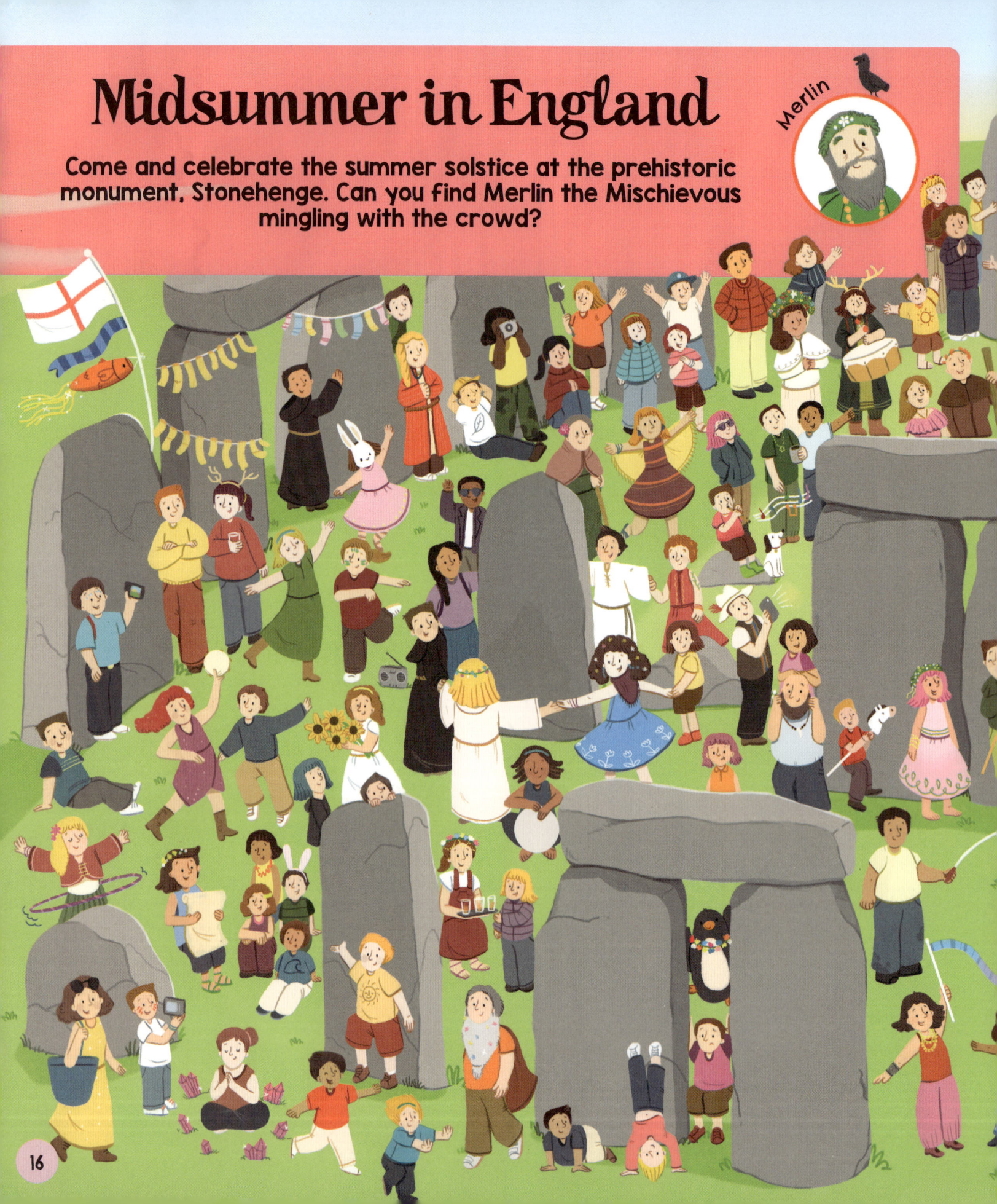

The Canals of Amsterdam

The capital of the Netherlands is famous for its winding canals and bright, tall buildings. Watch out for Vincenza Van Gotcha on your Dutch travels.

Vincenza

Northern Lights in Norway

Come and see the spectacular shimmering skies above Norway's glaciers. Where's Dorina the Dodger hiding?

Dorina

Floral Festivities in Poland

Float flower wreaths down the river, and enjoy the music and dancing of Wianki Festival in Kraków. Where's Agata Plan hiding?

Agata

Majestic Moscow

Get your skates on, and take to the ice rink at this winter wonderland in Russia's capital. Keep an eye out for Nikolai the Nimble.

Nikolai

Chinese New Year

Come and watch the world-famous festival of lanterns and light at Yuyuan Garden in Shanghai. Where's Secretive Shuchun lurking?

Shuchun

Have you spotted us?

Bustling India

Jump in a tuk-tuk, and weave your way through the busy traffic of Mumbai. Can you find Covert Kavitha?

Kavitha

Have you spotted us?

Waterways of Indonesia

Barter for a bargain at this floating fruit market in Borneo. Search for Mentari the Mystifying.

Mentari

Have you spotted us?

41

Beach Life in Oz

G'day from down under! Grab your diving gear, and explore the beautiful marine life of Australia's Great Barrier Reef. Can you spot Bewildering Bruce?

Bruce

Have you spotted us?

Animals of Africa

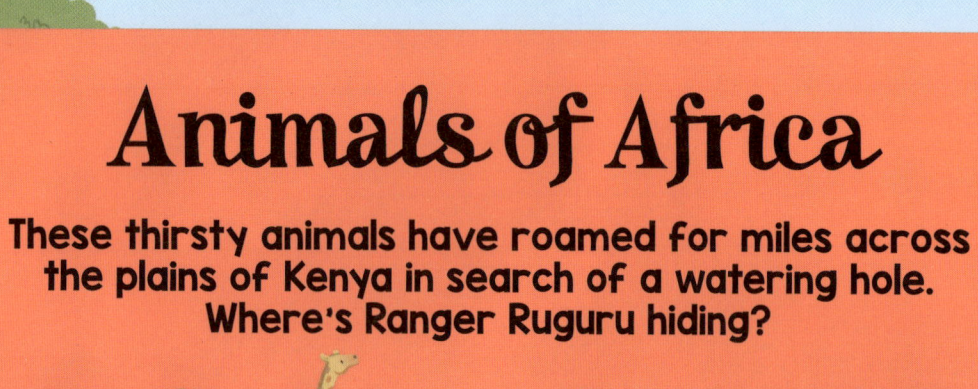

These thirsty animals have roamed for miles across the plains of Kenya in search of a watering hole. Where's Ranger Ruguru hiding?

Ruguru

Have you spotted us?

Pyramids of Giza

Inside these giant structures are the tombs of Ancient Egyptian royalty. Look out for mummies awoken from the dead! Can you find Clever Cleo?

Cleo

Have you spotted us?

Nigerian Street Market

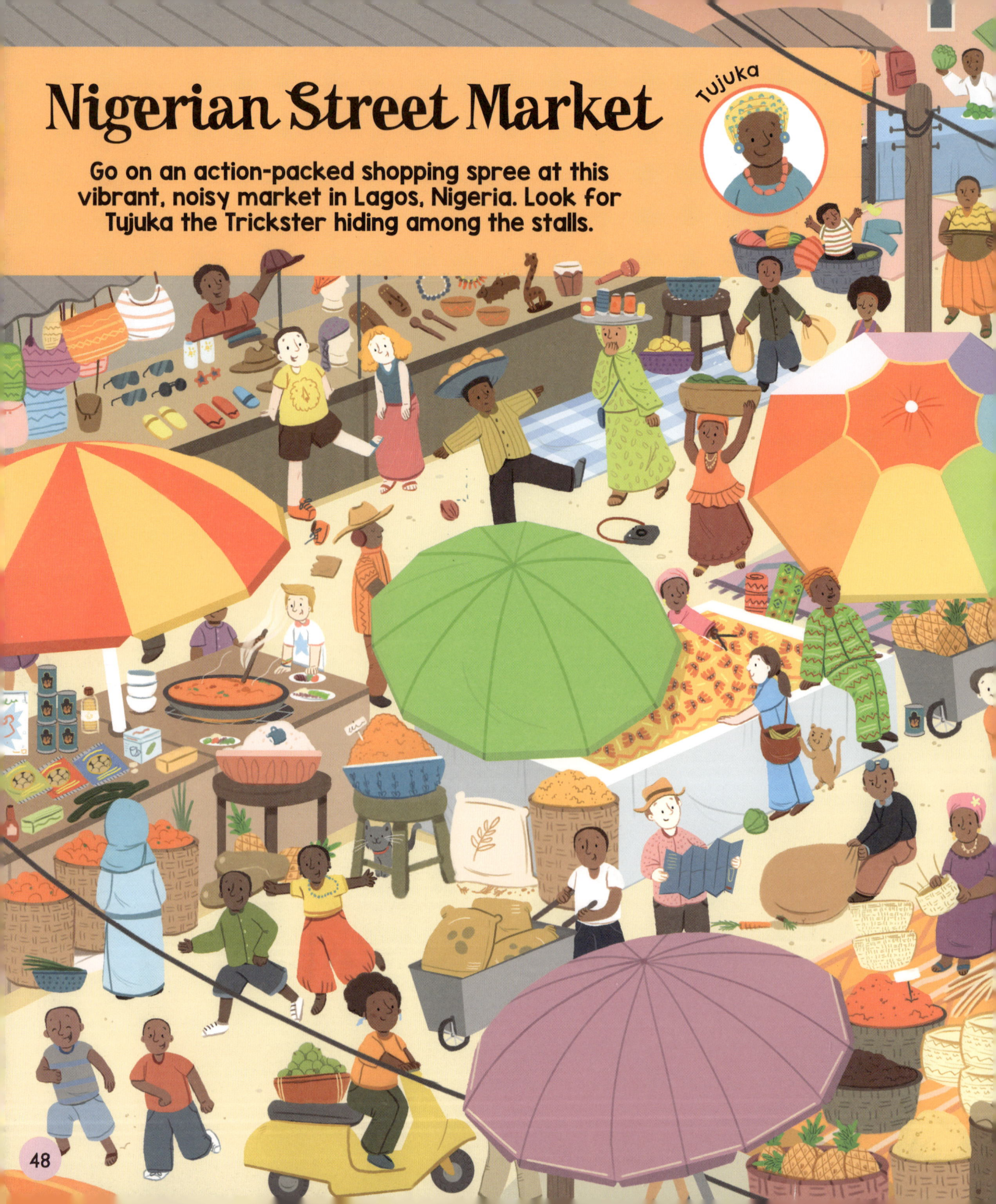

Go on an action-packed shopping spree at this vibrant, noisy market in Lagos, Nigeria. Look for Tujuka the Trickster hiding among the stalls.

Tujuka

Have you spotted us?

Tango Time in Argentina

Tap your feet to the beat, and dance the tango here in Buenos Aires, the birthplace of this lively dance. Can you spy Artful Arturo?

Arturo

Have you spotted us?

Picturesque Peru

Take in the panoramic views from Machu Picchu, the impressive city ruin nestled high in the Andes mountains. Where's Juanita Discreeta hiding?

Juanita

Have you spotted us?

Ecuadorian Expedition

The Amazon rain forest in South America is bursting with wondrous wildlife. Keep your eyes peeled for Faraway Fabio on your jungle adventure.

Fabio

Have you spotted us?

Football Frenzy in the USA

This popular American sport originated here in New Jersey. Which of these high school teams will you cheer on? Look for Olivia Obscura.

Olivia

Have you spotted us?

American Space School

These astronauts are training for their next mission here at America's space research HQ in Washington, DC. Can you see Inconspicuous Irene?

Irene

Have you spotted us?

Miami Beach

People flock to Florida, USA, to visit this glitzy beachside city, known for its sun, sand, and surf. Can you spot Mr. E?

Mr. E

Have you spotted us?

Texas Hoedown

Yee-haw! Welcome to the ranch. Swing your partner round and round at this barn dance in the Deep South of the USA. Where's Clandestine Clarabelle hiding?

Clarabelle

Have you spotted us?

Lake Life in Canada

Breathe in the fresh, pine-scented air, and marvel at Canada's spectacular wildlife, here in the Rocky Mountains. Can you spot Patrice the Pretender?

Patrice

64

Have you spotted us?

Shadow Match

Which of these silhouettes exactly matches the cheerleading formation?

A

B

C

D

E

F

66

Spot the Difference

Spot 10 differences between these two safari scenes.

67

Llama Logic

Which llama is the odd one out?

69

TOWERING TEASER

Fit the jigsaw pieces into the correct places. Which piece doesn't belong?

ARCADE ENIGMA

Which two claw machines are exactly the same?

MIAMI MEMORY PUZZLE

Study this scene for two minutes, then turn to the next page and answer the questions without looking back.

73

Miami Memory Puzzle

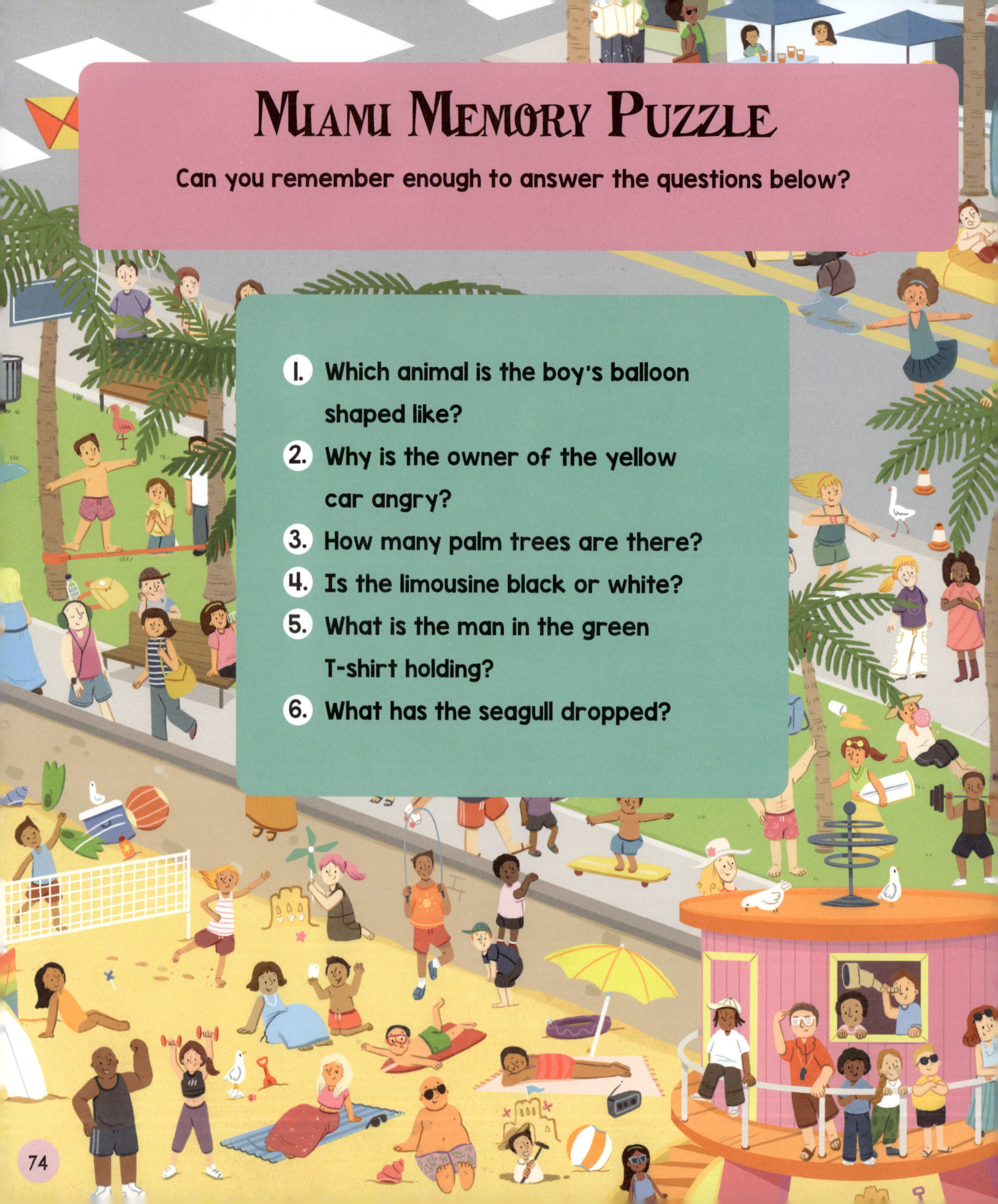

Can you remember enough to answer the questions below?

1. Which animal is the boy's balloon shaped like?
2. Why is the owner of the yellow car angry?
3. How many palm trees are there?
4. Is the limousine black or white?
5. What is the man in the green T-shirt holding?
6. What has the seagull dropped?

Dancing Shadows

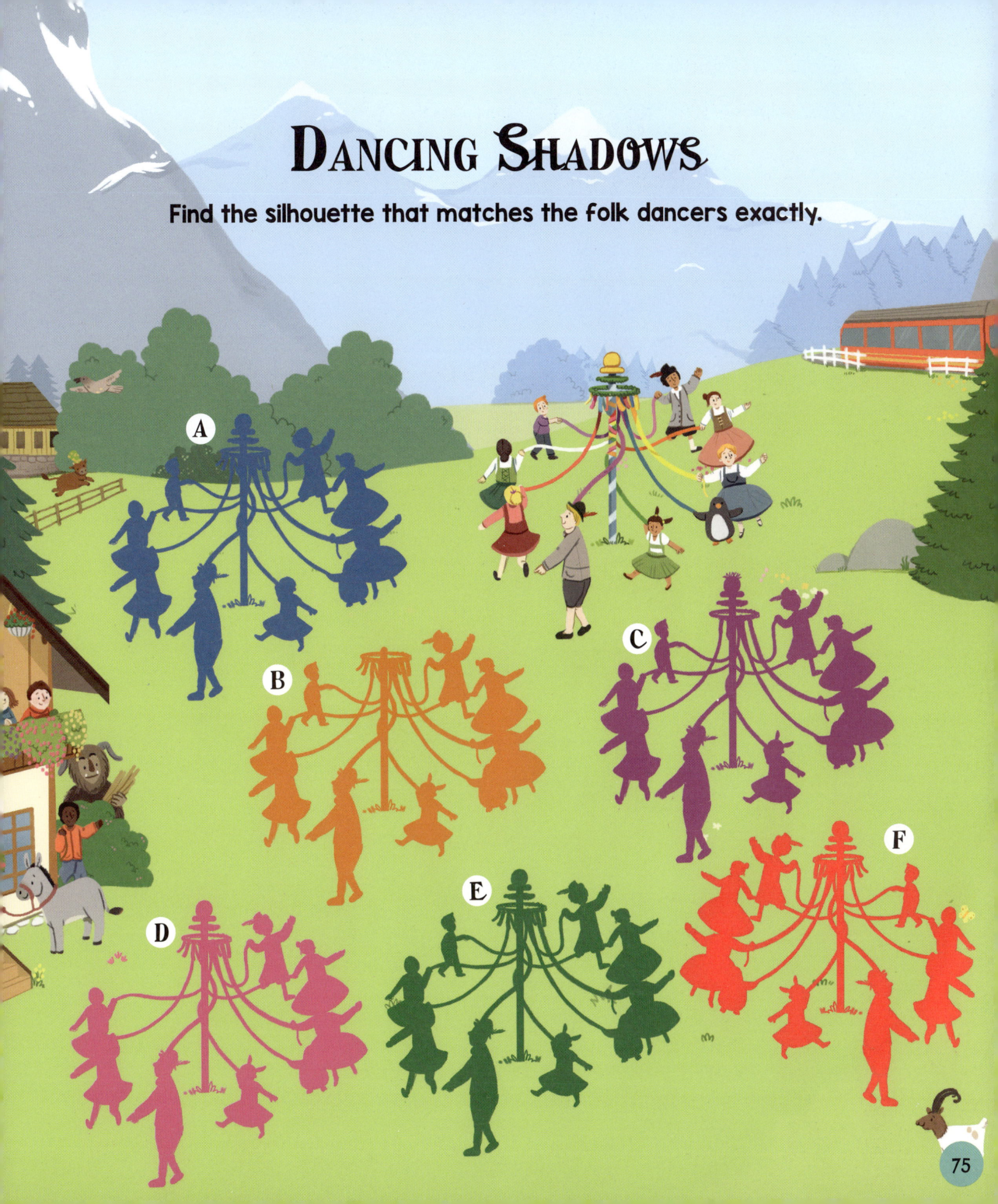

Find the silhouette that matches the folk dancers exactly.

DIVER DIFFERENCES

Spot 10 differences between these two scenes.

77

MARKET MAZE

Find your way through the floating market to the store.

Finish

Start

Paris Memory Puzzle

Study this scene for two minutes then turn the page to answer questions without turning back.

Paris Memory Puzzle

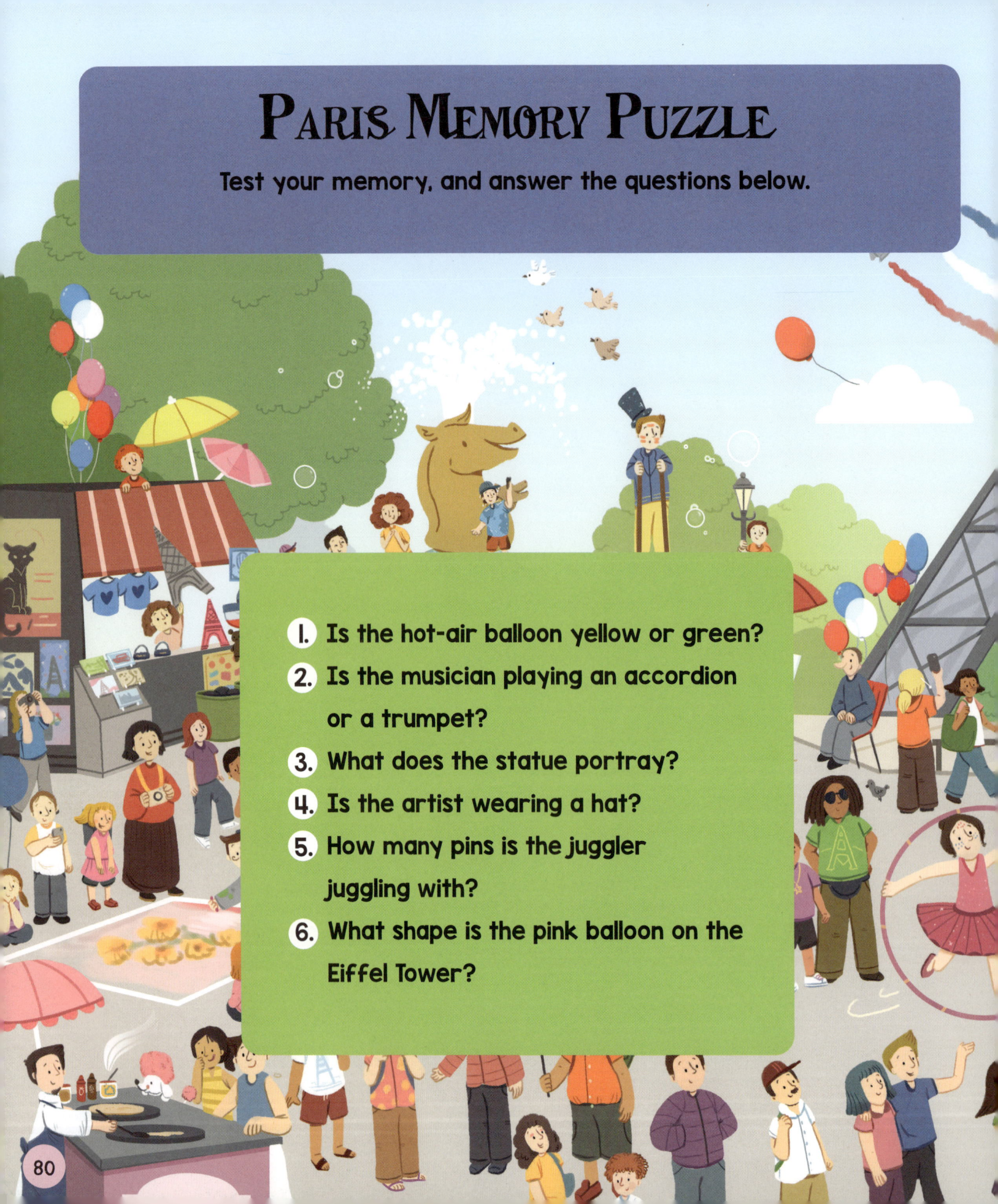

Test your memory, and answer the questions below.

1. Is the hot-air balloon yellow or green?
2. Is the musician playing an accordion or a trumpet?
3. What does the statue portray?
4. Is the artist wearing a hat?
5. How many pins is the juggler juggling with?
6. What shape is the pink balloon on the Eiffel Tower?

Flag Finder

Match each person to their country.

Japan

Canada

Norway

Russia

Egypt

Floating Fleet

Can you find two boats that look exactly the same?

83

FRUITY FIT

Complete the scene by fitting the jigsaw pieces into the correct places. Which piece doesn't belong?

WILDLIFE WANDERERS

Find five animals who don't belong in the Amazon rain forest.

CELTIC CONUNDRUM

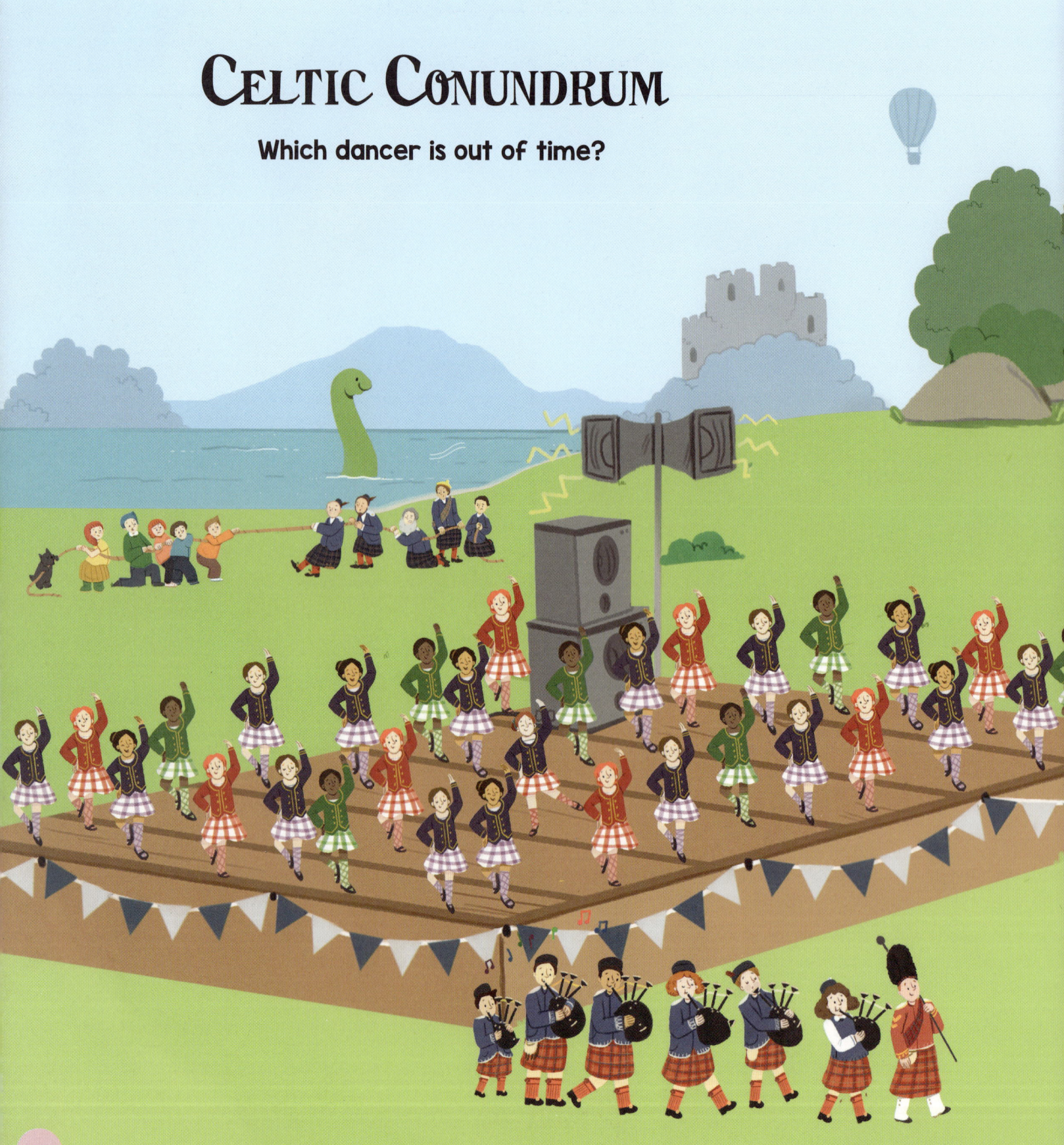

Which dancer is out of time?

86

Oasis Orienteering

Lead the camel over the bridges to water in the hot, dry desert. Watch out for scorpions and mummies!

Start

Finish

LIGHT UP THE SKY

Can you spot:
- 1 fish
- 2 rockets
- 3 purple flowers
- 4 butterflies
- 5 red lanterns

Answers

Pages 4-5 Fashionistas in France

Pages 6-7 Italian Feast

Pages 8-9 Food Fight in Spain

Pages 10-11 Party in Portugal

Pages 12-13 Ceilidh in Ireland

Pages 14-15 Scottish Games

Pages 16-17 Midsummer in England

Pages 18-19 The Canals of Amsterdam

Pages 20-21 Delightful Denmark

Pages 22-23 Cologne Carnival

Pages 24-25 Austrian Alps

Pages 26-27 Northern Lights in Norway

Pages 28-29 Swedish Ice Hotel

Pages 30-31 Floral Festivities in Poland

Pages 32-33 Majestic Moscow

Pages 34-35 High-Tech Tokyo

Pages 36-37 Chinese New Year

Pages 38-39 Bustling India

91

Pages 40-41 Waterways of Indonesia

Pages 42-43 Beach Life in Oz

Pages 44-45 Animals of Africa

Pages 46-47 Pyramids of Giza

Pages 48-49 Nigerian Street Market

Pages 50-51 Tango Time in Argentina

92

Pages 52-53 Picturesque Peru

Pages 54-55 Ecuadorian Expedition

Pages 56-57 Football Frenzy in the USA

Pages 58-59 American Space School

Pages 60-61 Miami Beach

Pages 62-63 Texas Hoedown

93

Pages 64-65 Lake Life in Canada

Page 66 Shadow Match

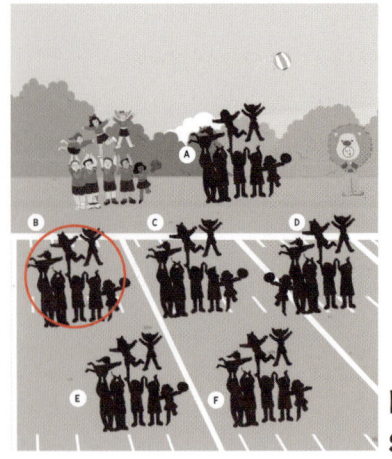

B is the matching silhouette.

Pages 67 Spot the Difference

Pages 68-69 Llama Logic

D is the odd one out.

Page 70 Towering Teaser

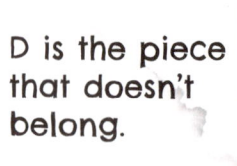

D is the piece that doesn't belong.

Page 71 Arcade Enigma

94

Page 74 Miami Beach Memory Puzzle

1. The boy's balloon is shaped like a dolphin.
2. The owner of the yellow car is angry because a pelican has pooped on his car.
3. There are four palm trees.
4. The limousine is black.
5. The man in the green T-shirt is holding a map.
6. The seagull has dropped ice cream.

Page 75 Dancing Shadows

E is the matching silhouette.

Pages 76-77 Diver Differences

Page 78 Market Maze

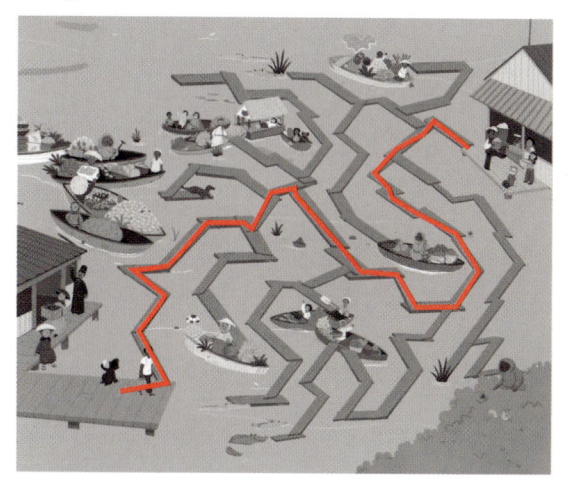

Page 80 Paris Memory Puzzle

1. The hot-air balloon is green.
2. The musician is playing the accordion.
3. The statue is a horse.
4. Yes, the artist is wearing a hat.
5. The juggler is juggling with six pins.
6. The pink balloon is heart shaped.

Page 81 Flag Finder

A — The Mountie on his horse is from Canada.
B — The lady in a folk dress is from Russia.
C — The reindeer herder is from Norway.
D — The pharaoh is from the Egypt.
E — The lady wearing a kimono is from Japan.

Pages 82-83 Floating Fleet

Page 84 Fruity Fit

G is the piece that doesn't belong.

Page 85 Wildlife Wanderers

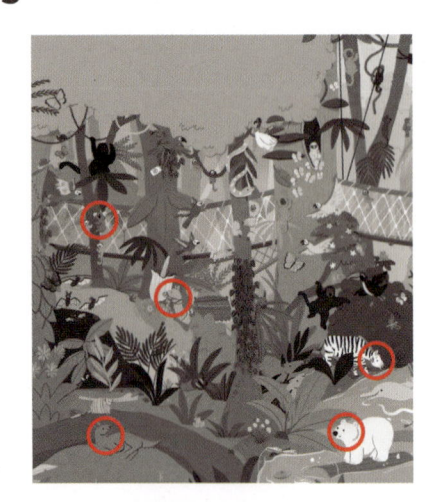

Page 86 Celtic Conundrum

Page 87 Oasis Orienteering

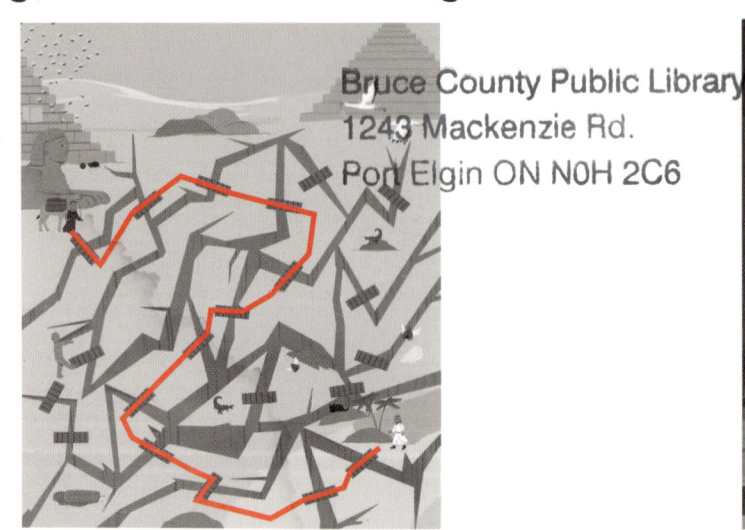

Page 88 Light up the Sky